First published in Belgium and Holland by Clavis Uitgeverij, Hasselt – Amsterdam, 2014
Copyright © 2014, Clavis Uitgeverij

English translation from the Dutch by Clavis Publishing Inc. New York
Copyright © 2015 for the English language edition: Clavis Publishing Inc. New York

Visit us on the web at www.clavisbooks.com

Mack's World of Wonder. Celebrations written and illustrated by Mack.
Original title: *Wondere wereld. Zo vieren wij feest*
Translated from the Dutch by Clavis Publishing

ISBN 978-1-60537-249-5

This book was printed in August 2015 at Proost Industries NV, Everdongenlaan 23, 2300 Turnhout, Belgium

First Edition
10 9 8 7 6 5 4 3 2 1

Mack's
world of
WONDER

CELEBRATIONS

Mack

Clavis

NEW YORK

HIP, HIP, HURRAY!
CELEBRATIONS

Hurray, a baby has been born! For nine months a baby grows in the mother's belly. When it is born, people bring presents like soft toys, books, or very small clothes. When you visit a newborn baby you might get a present too. Cookies, sugar coated almonds and aniseed candies called comfits are some traditional gifts. Yummy, they're delicious! The comfits are usually pink if the baby is a girl, and blue if it's a boy.

Which cupcake is for a boy, which one for a girl, and which one for a twin?

Not everyone celebrates the birth of a baby with cookies and comfits. On the island of Bali, in Indonesia, people welcome a baby with incense, water, flowers, and fruit. Women carry the flowers on their heads. But they wait to celebrate until the baby is a few months old. Until that time, the baby's feet can't touch the ground. In villages in the Philippines, mothers wash their child in the river immediately after they are born.

Flowers and fruit for a baby on the island Bali.

In the Philippines mothers wash their newborn children in the river.

Which baby is from the Philippines?

What is the best day of the year? That would have to be your birthday! At school and at home everyone sings "Happy Birthday," and you get nice presents. The whole room is decorated with ribbons and balloons for your party and there might be even lemonade and cake. The candles on the cake show how old the birthday boy or girl is. If you're turning four, there are four candles on the cake. Before you can eat the cake, you have to blow out all the candles. Make a wish as you blow!

When the piñata breaks, candy and confetti comes out. Hurray!

In South America no one celebrates a birthday without a piñata. The piñata is a doll or a decorated ball made of papier-mâché. It hangs in a tree or from the ceiling and is filled with confetti and candy. The birthday boy or girl tries to smash the piñata with a stick. That should be easy, but it isn't if you can't see! And the birthday child is blindfolded, so it can take a while to burst the piñata. But when it does – yummy – it rains candy, confetti, and streamers!

You probably think about birthdays as the day someone was born. But you can also celebrate other birthdays – like the birthday of a building or a country, or an event. Those birthdays are called anniversaries. The day the queen of England had been queen for sixty years, her anniversary was celebrated all over the country. The guards put on their finest clothes, the palace was beautifully decorated, and people danced and sang all night long.

The queen's palace was lit in different colors.

The guards let the canons boom.

Which person is the queen?

Ten, nine, eight, seven, six, five, four, three, two, one...

It's just before midnight on December 31, and everyone is counting down the seconds. Because at midnight sharp the new year begins. When the clock strikes twelve, fireworks burst and champagne corks pop. Happy New Year! People raise their glasses and kiss each other. And then they watch fireworks together. Wow, it's so pretty!

In New York City, many people celebrate New Year's Eve among the tall buildings and big video screens in Times Square.

At one minute before midnight it becomes clear what all the excitement is about. A big ball of light slowly drops from a tall building. At twelve o'clock sharp it reaches the ground and fireworks go off all over the city. *Happy New Year everyone!*

In China they don't celebrate New Year on January 1st. They celebrate a few weeks later. It is the most important celebration of the year and lasts no less than two weeks! There is red everywhere, because in China that color stands for good luck, and there are dragon dances in every town and village. Everyone celebrates his or her birthday at Chinese New Year, even the animals! Chinese people also celebrate their birthdays on the day they were born. So that's two parties a year. What fun!

In China red is the color of good luck.

People write down their wishes and hang them up in the trees.

Chinese fireworks.

Which color dragon brings good luck?

I LIKE YOU A LOT
CELEBRATIONS

One day a year Mom and Dad get to be spoiled because it's Father's Day or Mother's Day. On those days they get to be taken care of from dawn till dusk. They are served breakfast in bed and they don't need to do the dishes or clean up. Of course Mom and Dad also get presents. Home-made presents! Their children secretly make pretty drawings, and they give them to the best mom and dad in the whole world!

Which bunch has the most flowers in it?

WORLD ANIMAL DAY

When do animals celebrate? Well, on World Animal Day of course!
It takes place on October 4th and on that day all animals in the world are
pampered. Rabbits get extra juicy carrots, dogs get yummy bones, and
cats get funny toys. Some teachers even let their students bring their pets
to class.

Which animal celebrates animal day with a delicious carrot?

MARRIAGE

When two people are in love and they decide to spend the rest of their lives together, they often get married. The wedding sometimes takes place at the local town hall, and sometimes at church. Either way, the bride and groom promise to take care of each other. Then they put beautiful wedding rings on each other's fingers. When they leave the church or the town hall, people cheer and throw rice or flowers. The bridal couple, together with their friends and families, celebrates with cake and dancing!

Bridesmaid.

What belongs at a wedding?

In India weddings last a few days. During the celebration they burn sweet-smelling incense, there is music, and the bride and groom wear garlands. They have the celebration first and then the ceremony.
The bride wears beautiful clothes, and she places a red dot on her forehead.

Japanese bride and groom in a Japanese garden.

At a Japanese wedding the bride and groom wear special wedding kimonos. The bride often wears a headdress. Sometimes the couple carries special sunshades to protect them against bad fortune. The wedding pictures are taken in a beautiful Japanese garden. The couple looks so lovely!

VALENTINE'S DAY

Valentine's Day, which takes place on February 14th, is a celebration of love. It's the day when people in love give each other flowers, cards or other gifts to show they love each other. If you don't have a partner, you can still celebrate Valentine's Day by sending cards to friends and parents to let them know you love them. If you're in love but you're too shy to tell the person, you can send a card without your name on it. A Valentine's card without a name is very exciting to get!

Valentine's cards tell people that you care for them!

Which card is a real Valentine's card?

HOLY CELEBRATIONS

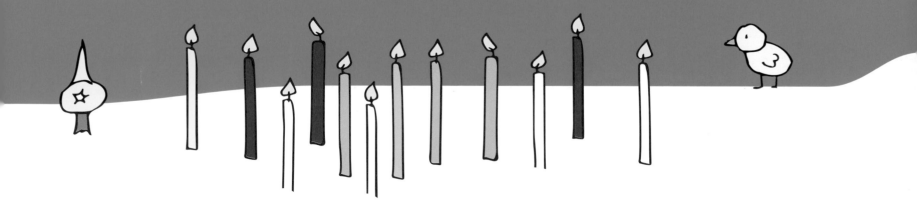

Every year on December 25th a lot of people celebrate the birth of Jesus. The story in the Bible tells us that Jesus was born a very long time ago in a stable in Bethlehem. That's why many people put a crèche under the Christmas tree. It shows baby Jesus sleeping in a crib of straw with his mother Mary and his father Joseph by his side. In the background there are cows and donkeys.

The star of Bethlehem.

The Christmas story in the Bible is beautiful. The angel Gabriel told Mary she would give birth to a special child, the Son of God. At first Mary didn't believe it, but it happened like the angel said it would. On the night Jesus was born, a star with a long tail appeared in the sky. That star pointed to the stable.

People often celebrate Christmas with their families. Everyone comes together on Christmas Eve and Christmas Day. The house is decorated with candles and garlands and decorations in Christmas colors – red, green, silver and gold. On Christmas Day everyone gathers for Christmas dinner. After a toast with wine or lemonade there is delicious food. Yummy!

It wouldn't be Christmas without a Christmas tree – a fir tree that stays nice and green in winter, too. People decorate their Christmas trees with beautiful decorations in all sorts of colors! Sometimes the trees outside are covered with lights too. In some countries the whole family wears party hats at Christmas, or hangs Christmas stockings at the fireplace. The stockings get filled with presents!

Easter is celebrated with bunnies, chicks, Easter baskets, and Easter egg hunts. Such fun! But do you know the reason we celebrate Easter? It's because Christians believe that Jesus rose from the dead on Easter. That is why the Pope gives a speech every year at Easter. The Friday before Easter is called Good Friday. That day silent processions are held to remember Jesus's death.

How many eggs have been hidden?

SUGAR FESTIVAL

At Sugar Festival Muslims celebrate the end of Ramadan. Ramadan is a month of fasting during which people visit each other and do good deeds. They don't eat or drink anything during the day. At the end of Ramadan there is a celebration, because the fasting is over. The whole family makes and eats the most delicious dishes and sweet treats. That is why this celebration is often called Sugar Festival.

Which pastries are decorated with a nut?

Loi Krathong, or the Festival of Light, is celebrated in Thailand. It is a celebration with water and little lights. Candles are lit and launched in the air in balloons. People also make small boats from the leaves of banana trees. The boats are shaped like lotus flowers and they are filled with decorations for the gods – and with candles, of course. People make wishes as they launch their boats on rivers, ponds, and canals.

This girl carefully puts her banana leaf boat into the water.

Which light animals do you see here?

Holi is a colorful festival. That's when Hindus celebrate the beginning of spring. If you walk around during Holi there's a good chance you will be sprinkled with perfume or colored water or powder. It's the way Hindus celebrate the return to color in nature after a gray winter. Holi is celebrated with dancing, singing, and delicious food. At the end of the festival people look like beautiful, colorful paintings.

Even the animals are colorful during Holi.

Which elephant didn't go to the Holi celebration?

CELEBRATIONS WITH A STORY

HALLOWEEN

Halloween is a fun and scary festival. In the past, people celebrated the end of harvest at Halloween time. That's why you still see so many pumpkins at Halloween. The only difference is that these pumpkins are scooped out to make lanterns with scary faces! Children dress up, then they knock on their neighbors' doors and call "Trick-or-treat!" Let's hope the neighbors aren't too scared, and they still give them some candy!

Name the witchy items you see here.

At carnival everyone dresses up! You see funny clowns, brave knights, graceful princesses, tough pirates and flexible super heroes walking around town. Everyone comes to the streets to watch the parade. Beautiful floats drive by one after the other. The people in the parade dance on the floats while they scatter colorful confetti all around. They scatter candy too! Carnival is such a fun feast!

Who is dressed as a cowboy? And who is dressed as a clown?

The biggest Carnival in the world is celebrated in Brazil. In the big city of Rio de Janeiro there is a contest between different districts to see who has made the best costumes and who is the best dancer. The Brazilians try very hard to win the contest. Men and women dance the samba to rhythmic music. They shake their hips and show off their beautiful costumes.

It is nice and warm in Brazil, so Carnival is celebrated on the beach.

Who has the most colorful headdress?

In Russia the end of winter is celebrated with a big party called Maslenitsa or Crepe Week. You can probably guess what that means: you eat a lot of crepes during this feast! Actually, they are called "blini" in Russia. They're like small pancakes. The Russians don't care that they are small, they just eat a few extra. At the end of the celebrations people burn a doll made of straw.

Burning a straw doll is how people say goodbye to winter.

Which crepes are decorated with delicious strawberries?

FUNFAIR

Once or twice a year the traveling funfair comes to town! The funfair is a sort of small amusement park. You can play games, or go for rides. Maybe, if you're brave enough, you can ride the bumper cars or go on the Ferris wheel that reaches high above the ground. If you like candy, you will definitely like the funfair. You can buy lollipops, sticks of rock candy, and cotton candy in all the colors of the rainbow.

Whose hair looks a bit like cotton candy?

In Sweden and Finland it almost never gets dark in the summer. Everyone looks forward to this season. Not just because the weather is warm and the sun shines for a very long time, but also because Midsummer's Eve Festival is celebrated. It's the best festival of the year! In Finland they light a big bonfire. In Sweden people dance around the maypole and girls wear garlands on their heads.

The maypole is decorated with leaves and flowers.

Which sheep celebrated Midsummer's Eve Festival?

Thanksgiving takes place in the United States and Canada to celebrate the harvest and to give thanks for the food we have to eat. The whole family gathers together and eats a delicious feast of roast turkey, cranberry sauce, and pumpkin pie. We give thanks, not only for the food, but for all the things that make us grateful, including the family and friends who are sharing the meal.

Which birds are turkeys and which are chickens?